NEWMAN THE HUMAN

Written by Andrea W. Meyer

Illustrated by Mayra Viney

Moon • Clover

PUBLISHING

For my boys. –A.W.M.

For my husband and all of our beautiful children. –M.V.

A special thank you to our friend, Rachel Goodell,
for editing our book.

This book belongs to:

Glossary:

Spaceship: A spaceship is a vehicle that you can zip, zoom, and vroom in while traveling all over the galaxy.

Moon: Moons are smaller bodies that orbit, or circle around, larger bodies, such as planets or asteroids. Earth has one moon.

Asteroid: Asteroids are very large, rocky objects that travel through space.

Star: A star is a huge ball of light and heat at the center of a solar system. The star nearest to Earth is the Sun.

Galaxy: A galaxy is a collection of billions of stars and their solar systems, as well as gas and dust. You, Newman, and Blorg live in the Milky Way galaxy.

Jupiter: Jupiter is the largest planet in our solar system. It is so big that all the other planets in our solar system could fit inside it! It is close to where Blorg and his friends live.

Alien: An alien is a being from a planet other than Earth. They love to play chase!

Newman the Human is a lucky boy,
though he doesn't have a dog, a frog, or even a toy.

He does have a spaceship
that can take him wherever he wants to go
– whether it's to the moon or all the way to Pluto.

But there is one thing Newman wishes he had:
a friend he could zip, zoom, and vroom with.
He wanted that so bad!

They would race around the asteroids
and jump over the moon.
They'd even snack behind the stars
and laugh all afternoon.

But flying around the galaxy,
he was all alone.
Newman had no friends
to call his own.

Then one day near Jupiter,
as he was bolting by,
Newman looked down
and saw someone waving "hi."

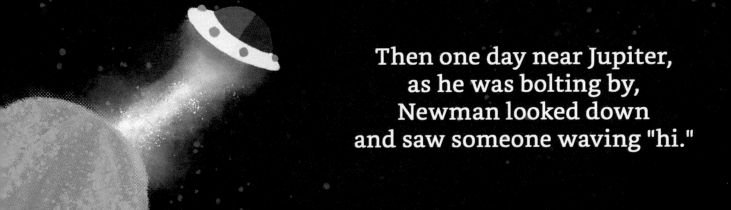

They certainly weren't human.
They looked nothing like Newman,
with their green skin, purple fins,
and all 20 of their eyes.

Newman quickly landed his ship,
hoping for new adventures on this trip.

"My name is Blorg," he said as he gathered his friends.
But his pals started laughing and pointing their fins!

"He only has two eyes
and no fins,"
they pointed out.

"And with only ten toes,
how can he run about?"

Newman said,
"I don't need fins
or extra toes to play chase –

Let's hop in our spaceships
and have a race!"

The aliens thought about it for a second,
and then for one more.

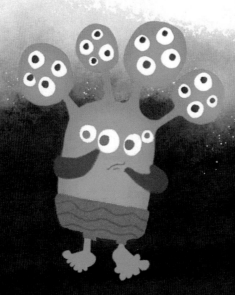

Then Blorg said,
"Come on, gang, let's blast off
with Newman and explore!"

"But first, I have a confession to make:
I only have ten toes, too. The rest are all fake."

Sparked by Blorg's honesty
to just be himself,
one alien said:
"I'm missing a fin.
This one is made of felt!"

"I only have 19 eyes,"
one said.
"This one here isn't even real."

"My skin isn't green,"
said another. "It's actually teal."

One by one, they revealed what they were hiding.
And you know what? It was kind of exciting!

Each alien was unique
and they thought that was neat.
They embraced all their differences –
even Newman's feet!

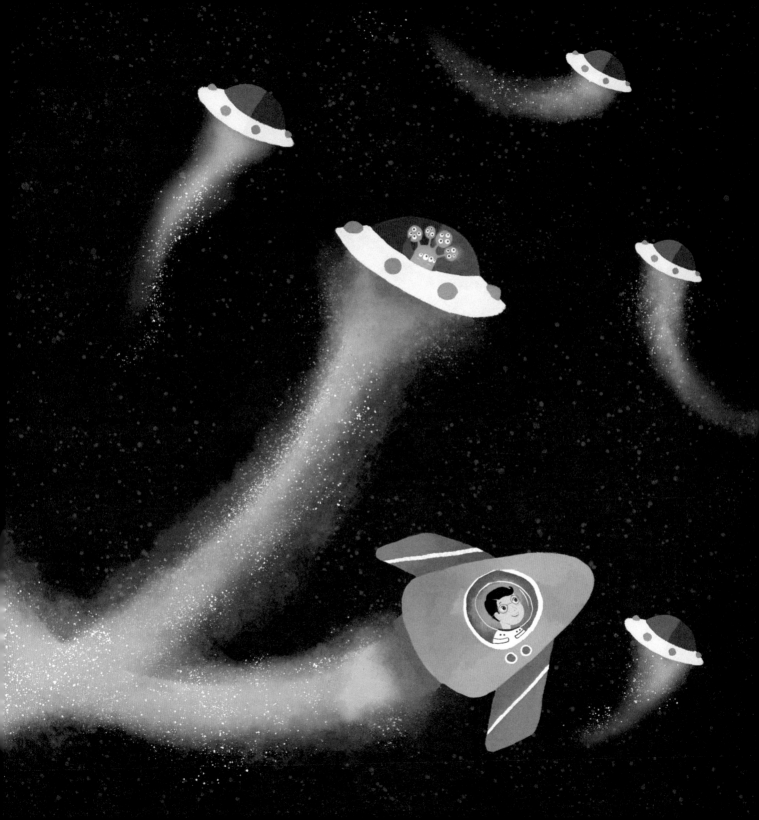

Andrea W. Meyer is a Texas-based author and former journalist. The Louisiana native wrote for television, print, and digital media before transitioning to the marketing sector, all the while maintaining her creative pursuits. She and her family enjoy mermaid watching in Galveston Bay and going on holiday with their cats to the moon. Newman the Human is her first children's book.

Mayra Viney is a multidisciplinary artist with experience creating using traditional and digital media. Newman the Human is the first book she has illustrated. The Texan native enjoys traveling and going to concerts with her family.

Made in the USA
Monee, IL
02 October 2021